FAMILIUS

Copyright © 2017 by Rino Alaimo

All rights reserved.

Published by Familius LLC, www.familius.com

Familius books are available at special discounts for bulk purchases, whether for sales promotions or for family or corporate use. For more information, contact Familius Sales at 559-876-2170 or email orders@familius.com.

Library of Congress Cataloging-in-Publication Data
2016953872
pISBN 9781944822804
eISBN 9781944822811

Cover and book design by David Miles
Author photograph copyright © Ilaria Franzese

10 9 8 7 6 5 4 3 2 1
First Edition
Printed in China

Like a Shooting Star

Rino Alaimo

The war had just ended.

The nights, once filled by the silence of fear, now rustled with the hope that soldiers sent to fight in distant lands could return home to hug their loved ones.

During those nights of prayer and waiting, most children snuggled in bed to dream of their brave fathers and mothers. But there was one child, just the one, who sat outside instead. All night long, the boy held tight to a picture of his father and watched the sky for a shooting star.

If only a star would fall! He could make a wish and his father would return safely home.

Very near the place where the boy spent his sleepless nights, there was a bush filled with fireflies. Each night they danced in the warm wind and flew under the stars.

But the tiniest of them just couldn't fly. Again and again she leapt into the air, but again and again she fell to the ground while the other fireflies pointed and teased.

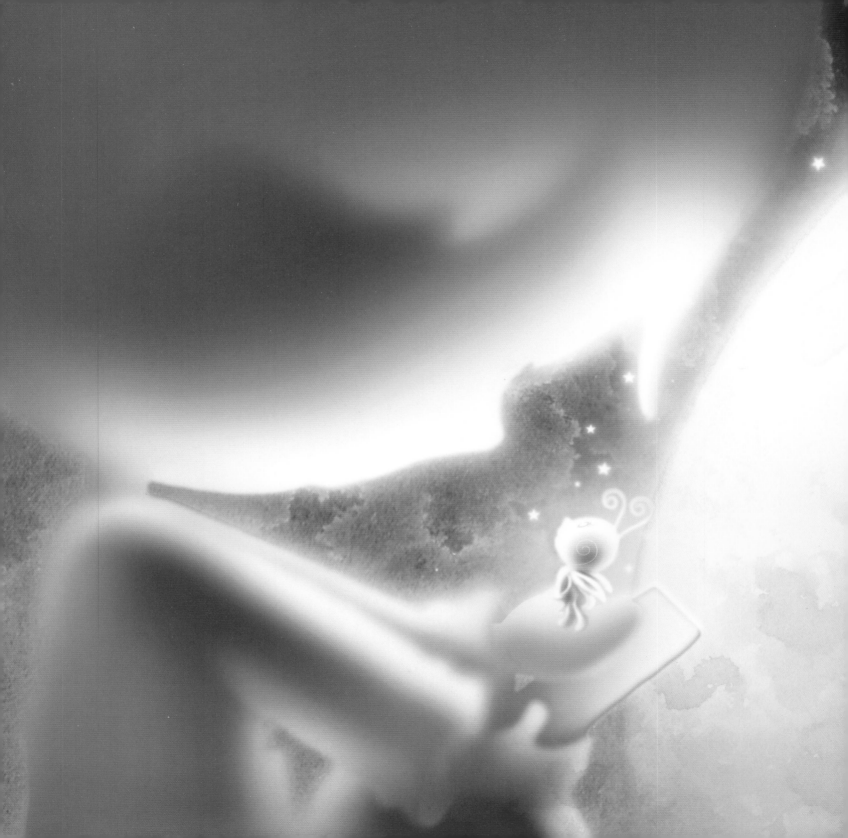

One night, the Firefly gave a mighty leap and launched herself up, up, up into the sky. But instead of falling back to her bush, she fell far away into the hands of the little boy.

"Oh, light from heaven," said the boy. "You must be a star. I have waited many nights to tell you my wish. Please, can you bring my father home safely from the war?"

He showed the Firefly the picture of his father.

The boy's plea touched the firefly. For the first time, she felt strong and confident in herself. "I can't fly," she whispered, "but I promise I'll bring your father home."

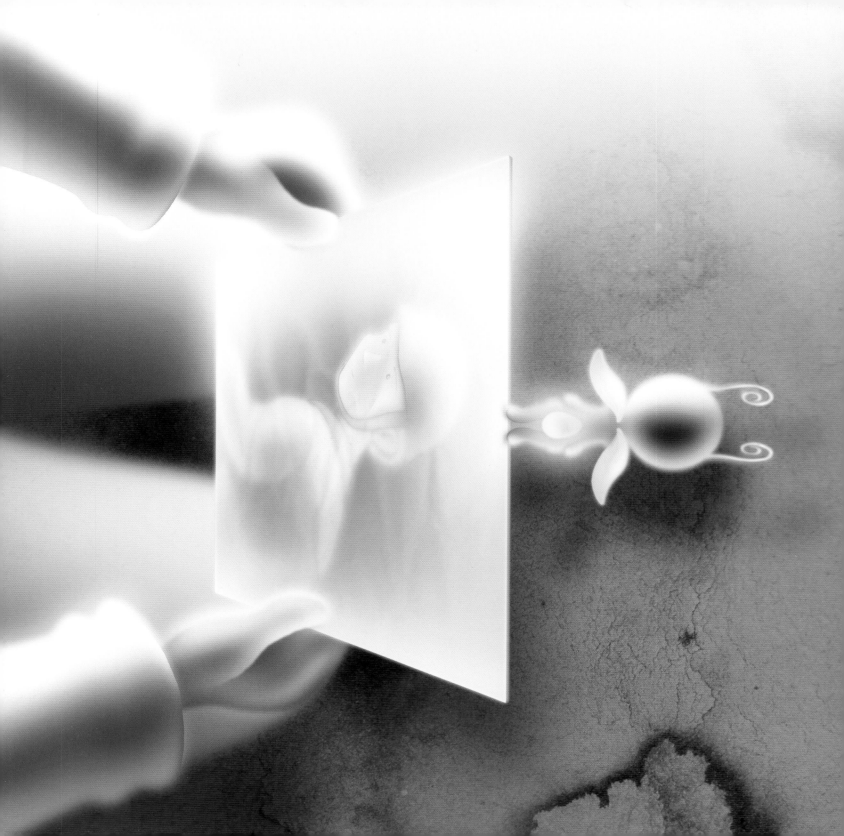

She looked at the picture of the boy's father and carefully studied his face. Then, like a tiny pebble skipped across a stream, she bounced away and disappeared into the night.

First, she looked for the boy's father on land, searching all of the trains that carried soldiers home.

But she did not find him.

She looked for him on the waves of the sea,
searching all the boats carrying soldiers home.

But she did not find him.

She looked for him high in the skies, clinging to the wing of an airplane and studying the faces of all the soldiers loaded inside.

But still, she did not find him.

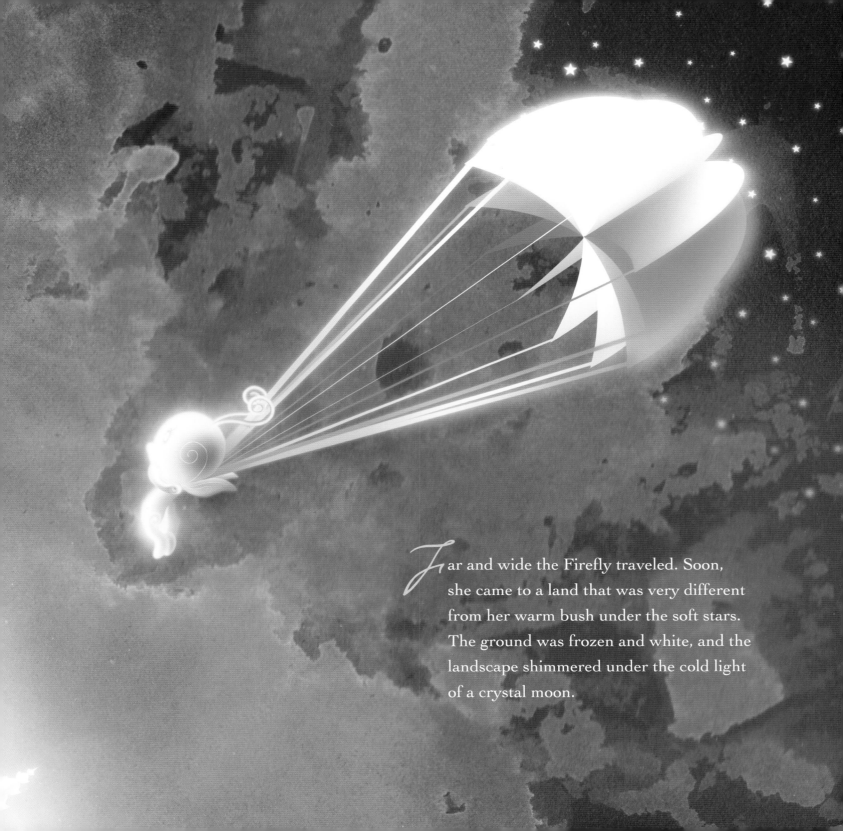

$\mathcal{F}$ar and wide the Firefly traveled. Soon, she came to a land that was very different from her warm bush under the soft stars. The ground was frozen and white, and the landscape shimmered under the cold light of a crystal moon.

Nearby, hidden in the sea of white, was a lonely, tired soldier. He had lost his
way in the snow and had fallen behind his company.

But just as his hope was fading, a small spark of light appeared. The soldier stood up in wonder as the light bounced toward him. It reminded him of the fireflies back home. But of course, fireflies cannot live in snowy places. And they certainly don't bounce . . . do they?

The Firefly looked into the soldier's face and saw the little boy's father.

"I've found you!" she cried in her tiny voice. "Your boy wished that I would find you and bring you home. I've found you! Come, follow me."

The soldier couldn't believe what he heard, but he thought of his little boy and felt the child's wish warm him from his helmet to his boots with new strength.

For many days and nights they traveled, on and on over the highest mountains and across the deepest seas. But no matter how tired they were, the Firefly burned her little light and led the soldier home.

Soon the breeze filled with a new smell. It wasn't mud or gunpowder. It was the scent of laundry and clean soap—the sweet, familiar, wonderful smell of home that meant it was time to cast off the soldier's uniform.

The boy saw his father enter the door and leapt into his arms.

"I knew you'd come!" he cried with delight. "I wished on a shooting star."

They hugged tightly and looked into each other's eyes for a long, long time.

The little Firefly watched from outside the window. Joy raced through her heart and love beat in her wings. She lit up the sky with happiness, and it was a long time before she realized something else: